CLEAN UP, GRUMPY BUNNY!

For Candace Miller Rice,
inventor of the Millerian Principles of Neatness
—J.K.F.

For little Miss Molly
—Love, Lucy

ISBN-13: 978-0-439-87381-9
ISBN-10: 0-439-87381-9

Text copyright © 2006 by Justine Korman Fontes.
Illustrations copyright © 2006 by Lucinda McQueen.
All rights reserved. Published by Scholastic Inc.
SCHOLASTIC, CARTWHEEL BOOKS, and associated logos are
trademarks and/or registered trademarks of Scholastic Inc.

12 11 10 9 8 7 6 5 4 3 2 1   7 8 9 10 11 12/0

Printed in the U.S.A.   23
This edition first printing, February 2007

CLEAN UP, GRUMPY BUNNY!

by Justine Korman Fontes
Illustrated by Lucinda McQueen

SCHOLASTIC INC.

New York   Toronto   London   Auckland   Sydney
Mexico City   New Delhi   Hong Kong   Buenos Aires

Chapter 1
Mr. Mess

Hopper O'Hare was messy.

He took out many toys during playtime.
But Hopper never put any away.

Playtime was over.
"Clean up!" said Mrs. Clover.
But Hopper did not.

"Aren't you going to help?"
asked Corny.
"I'm busy reading!" Hopper said.
"You're always busy during cleanup,"
Corny said.
But Hopper just went back to reading
his book.

"It isn't fair!" Marigold cried.
"Hopper makes the biggest mess.
But he never cleans up."
"Why should we clean up
Hopper's mess?" Corny said.
"You're right," Mrs. Clover said.
"Hopper should clean up, too."

"You will miss hippety-hop practice
if you don't start cleaning up,"
Mrs. Clover said.

Hopper didn't listen.
No one ever missed hippety-hop!
Hippety-hop was even more important
than painting eggs or making baskets.

Chapter 2
Clean Up...or Else!

Mrs. Clover told the other bunnies
not to clean up for Hopper.

"Please begin your hippety-hops
while Hopper cleans up," she said.

"Me? Clean up? All alone?"
Hopper asked.
"Yes," Mrs. Clover said.
"You'll have to miss hippety-hop
until you learn to clean up."
"Oh, worms!" Hopper cried.
"I hate cleaning up!"

Mrs. Clover patted his shoulder.
"Cleaning up after yourself is
part of growing up," she said.
"Wiggly worms on toast,"
Hopper said.

Then Lilac Lapin raised her paw.
"May I help Hopper? I like cleaning up."
Mrs. Clover agreed.

Hopper couldn't believe his ears.
"How can anyone like cleaning up?"
"Cleaning up is a game," Lilac explained.

Chapter 3
The Game

"I pretend I'm a librarian when I put away books," she said.

"Being a librarian would be fun,"
Hopper said. "Then I could read
all the books I want."
Soon Hopper and Lilac had put away
all the books.

"I like to put away cars," Lilac said.
"I pretend I run a parking garage."

Hopper handed Lilac a truck.
"Beep! Beep! Make room for a big one,"
he said.
Soon all the toy trucks and cars were
neatly parked.

"Now let's put all the friends together," Lilac said.
"Friends?" Hopper asked.
Lilac giggled. "I pretend things that are alike are friends. Blocks belong with blocks, robots with robots..."

"I get it!" Hopper shouted. "Friends are happier when they're together," Lilac said. "So cleaning up is a happy thing."

Hopper put a T. rex on the shelf with the
other dinosaurs.
"Now you won't be lonely," he told the toy.
Hopper giggled.
Lilac laughed, too.

Then, they rounded up the toy horses.
Hopper smiled. "I hope they'll be happy
at the Big Shelf Ranch."

"I like to put little things in front
of big things," Lilac said.
"That way the little ones won't
miss the view."

She tucked a little teddy bear
on the shelf.
"Now he can see everything,"
Hopper said.

Chapter 4
Chore No More

"Cleaning up helps me find my toys," Lilac said.

Hopper held up a block.
"I have never seen this one before,"
he said. "It would make a cool cave
next time we play with blocks."

Hopper was almost sad when
they were done.

Then, he laughed.
"What's so funny?" Lilac asked.
"I can't wait to go home and clean up
my room!" Hopper said.

Mrs. Clover thanked Hopper and Lilac
for doing a good job.
"I hope you'll clean up after yourself
from now on," she told Hopper.
"Cleaning up is way too much fun to skip!"
Hopper said.